The Forgotten Melody

Marquise The Coach

Published by Marquise The Coach, 2024.

This is a work of fiction. Similarities to real people, places, or events are entirely coincidental.

THE FORGOTTEN MELODY

First edition. April 9, 2024.

Copyright © 2024 Marquise The Coach.

ISBN: 979-8224366637

Written by Marquise The Coach.

A Forgotten Legacy

Elena Miller prided herself on being a pragmatist. Fairytales were for children, and hidden treasures belonged in dusty novels, not the cluttered attic of her recently deceased aunt.

Yet, there it was, nestled amongst moth-eaten scarves and faded photographs – a weathered trunk adorned with intricate brass clasps, whispering promises of a forgotten past.

A shiver danced down Elena's spine, a strange sense of anticipation taking root.

Could this be the key to unlocking a family secret?

Or a Pandora's box filled with shadows she'd rather leave undisturbed?

Turn the page to discover what lies within the trunk, and embark on a journey that blends the haunting melody of a hidden past with the vibrant rhythm of the present.

Chapter 1: The Unwanted Inheritance

***

Dust motes danced in the afternoon sunlight filtering through the grimy attic window.

Elena Miller coughed, pulling her scarf tighter around her nose and mouth.

The air hung heavy with the scent of forgotten memories – mothballs, old leather, and a faint trace of lavender that sent a shiver down her spine.

Cleaning out her Aunt Clara's house was a bittersweet task.

Clara, the quirky spinster with a penchant for collecting oddities, had passed away peacefully a few months ago, leaving the ramshackle Victorian to Elena, her only living relative.

Now, amidst the clutter of a life well-lived, Elena felt a pang of loneliness.

Clara had been a constant presence, a source of erratic advice and endless cups of chamomile tea. Without her, the silence in the house felt deafening.

Elena pushed a stray cobweb clinging to a dusty gramophone aside, her gaze sweeping over the seemingly endless piles of forgotten treasures.

There were chipped porcelain dolls with lifeless eyes, a collection of mismatched teacups, and a stack of National Geographic magazines from the 1950s.

In the corner, shrouded in a white sheet, stood a dusty grandfather clock with its hands forever frozen at ten past three.

Elena knew each object held a story, a fragment of Clara's life she never fully shared.

As she continued, a lone, ornately carved trunk tucked beneath a stack of old trunks caught her eye.

Unlike the others, it was made of a dark, rich wood, its brass clasps intricately designed with swirling floral patterns.

A sense of curiosity, a feeling like a forgotten melody stirring in the recesses of her mind, drew Elena towards it.

Kneeling beside the trunk, she ran her fingers across the cool metal, tracing the intricate design.

It was heavier than she expected, and the clasps seemed stubbornly resistant.

With a grunt and a determined twist, they finally yielded.

A rush of stale air wafted out, carrying the scent of aged wood and something else, something she couldn't quite place.

Inside, nestled amongst moth-eaten scarves and faded photographs, lay a violin case.

Elena, who had always harbored a secret love for music despite leaving it behind years ago, felt a tug at her heart.

The case was worn leather, the color of deep burgundy, and a silver nameplate tarnished with age read simply: "A. Hartmann."

Beside it lay a leather-bound journal, its pages yellowed with time.

An inscription on the inner cover sent a jolt of electricity through her: "Amelia Hartmann, 1938." The name jolted a memory loose.

Clara had once mentioned a distant relative, a great-aunt who lived in Vienna. Could this be...?

Intrigued, Elena carefully opened the violin case.

The instrument itself was a thing of beauty, its wood a deep, polished amber with a gentle curve that seemed to beckon her touch.

A small, folded piece of paper lay tucked under the velvet lining.

Elena unfolded it, revealing a handwritten message scrawled in a flowing script.

It was a series of musical notes, unlike anything she'd ever seen, their configuration both elegant and strangely unsettling.

Holding the violin and the journal in her hands, Elena felt an undeniable connection to this woman from the past.

Who was Amelia Hartmann, and what secrets did this violin hold?

As she traced the faded notes with her finger, Elena knew she was about to embark on a journey that would not only unlock the mysteries of the past but also force her to confront a passion she had long denied.

This dusty attic trunk, filled with forgotten treasures, had become a gateway to a story buried for generations, a melody waiting to be played.

Chapter 2: Echoes in Sheet Music

The weight of the violin case felt heavy in Elena's hands as she descended the creaking attic stairs.

The faded musical notes tucked inside the case were like a puzzle waiting to be solved, a melody yearning to be heard.

Back in Clara's cluttered living room, she settled onto the worn floral couch, the violin case resting on her lap.

Sunlight streamed through a dusty window, illuminating the intricate symbols scrawled on the paper.

These weren't standard musical notation.

The swirling lines and unfamiliar symbols resembled ancient hieroglyphics, defying easy comprehension.

Elena, despite years away from music, recognized a certain elegance in the arrangement.

A sense of frustration gnawed at her.

What did these notes represent?

A forgotten composition?

A cryptic message?

She rummaged through a drawer and retrieved her worn copy of music theory, hoping to find a clue.

Hours melted away as she compared the symbols on the paper to standard notation, searching for a pattern.

Disappointment clawed at her.

The notes seemed to defy all logic, a beautiful yet frustrating enigma.

Giving up for the moment, Elena picked up Amelia's journal.

The leather cover felt worn and smooth beneath her fingertips.

Tentatively, she unclasped the brass lock and inhaled the musty scent of aged paper.

The first few pages were filled with mundane entries – practice schedules, concert dates, and reviews from local newspapers.

Amelia, it seemed, was a rising star in Vienna's pre-war music scene, a violinist praised for her technical brilliance and emotional depth.

Suddenly, a faded photograph slipped out from between the pages.

It depicted a young woman, no older than Elena, with a head full of dark curls and a determined glint in her eyes.

She held a violin, its shape identical to the one in the case.

A pang of kinship shot through Elena. This was Amelia, the woman who once held this very instrument, the woman who wrote the cryptic music.

As Elena turned the page, a chill crawled down her spine. The familiar script was replaced with hurried scribbles, the ink dark and spidery.

Dates were interspersed with frantic phrases – "They're coming," "Nowhere to hide," and a chilling phrase in German, "Die Musik muss sterben" – The music must die. Horror welled up inside Elena.

What had happened to Amelia?

Why was the music considered a threat?

The afternoon light began to fade, casting long shadows across the room.

Elena slammed the journal shut, a sense of foreboding settling in her stomach. The cryptic notes, the desperate journal entries – they all hinted at a dark secret, a story waiting to be unearthed.

For the first time, Elena realized that traversing into Amelia's past wasn't just about curiosity. It was about unraveling a truth that had been buried for generations, a truth that might change everything.

Chapter 3: Whispers of a Lost City

The days that followed were a whirlwind of research and frustration. Elena devoured every scrap of information she could find about pre-war Vienna.

The city, once a vibrant hub of music and culture, seemed to hold the key to Amelia's story. But the internet proved a labyrinth of conflicting information and historical whitewashing.

Frustrated, Elena decided to visit the local music conservatory, a grand stone building with an air of hushed reverence.

Inside, the scent of aged wood and polished brass mingled with the faint strains of a cello practicing scales.

She found herself in a dusty library, the walls lined with ancient leather-bound scores and faded concert posters.

A kindly librarian with twinkling eyes and a shock of white hair listened patiently as Elena explained her predicament. "The notes you have," she mused, her voice a gentle rasp, "they don't resemble any traditional notation I've seen. Could they be some kind of code?"

Elena's heart leaped.

"A code? But who would use music for a code?"

The librarian smiled faintly.

"Espionage during wartime often resorted to creative methods. Music, with its complex structures and hidden meanings, could be an ideal way to transmit secret messages."

A cold dread settled in Elena's stomach.

Was this what Amelia's notes represented?

A secret message hidden in plain sight?

The librarian suggested contacting Professor Strauss, a retired musicologist with a deep knowledge of pre-war music.

Elena tracked down Professor Strauss, a frail man with a stooped posture and a gaze clouded by age.

His apartment, filled with dusty manuscripts and overflowing bookshelves, felt like a museum of forgotten melodies.

He spent hours poring over the sheet music, his brow furrowed in concentration.

"These notes are unlike anything I've encountered," he finally admitted, his voice raspy. "The style hints at a specific school of composition banned by the Nazis. It could be a form of protest music, a defiance against the regime."

He explained the rise of Nazi Germany and its suppression of art deemed "degenerate."

Jewish composers and musicians were ostracized, their works banned or destroyed.

A terrifying picture began to form in Elena's mind.

Could Amelia have been harboring a Jewish composer?

Was the music a protest song, a hidden cry against oppression?

Professor Strauss, despite his failing memory, offered a glimmer of hope.

He suggested contacting the Vienna Historical Society, a group dedicated to preserving the city's wartime history.

With a renewed sense of purpose, Elena booked a flight to Vienna, the city of music and shadows, determined to unravel the secrets buried within Amelia's past.

Chapter 4: A City of Contrasts

The plane touched down in Vienna with a soft thud, pulling Elena out of her reverie. Stepping out of the terminal, she was greeted by a crisp autumn breeze and a cityscape that seemed to exist in two distinct timelines.

Grand, Baroque buildings with ornate facades stood shoulder-to-shoulder with sleek, modern skyscrapers.

The air crackled with a vibrant energy, an almost jarring contrast to the weight of history she carried within her.

Following a map scrawled on a crumpled piece of paper, Elena found her way to a charming pension tucked away on a cobblestone street.

The proprietor, a woman with wrinkles like laughter lines around her eyes, greeted her with a warm smile and a cup of strong Viennese coffee.

After checking in, Elena stepped out onto the balcony overlooking the street. Below, people bustled along, their laughter and chatter forming a familiar symphony. It was hard to reconcile this peaceful scene with the horrors Amelia had likely witnessed.

The Vienna Historical Society was housed in a stately building on Ringstrasse, a grand boulevard lined with historical landmarks.

Elena was greeted by Dr. Schmidt, a young historian with keen eyes and an air of quiet determination.

"The music you have," Dr. Schmidt said after examining the sheet music, "it does resemble the banned style of composers like Arnold Schoenberg.

It's possible Amelia was harboring a Jewish musician during the war."

Elena recounted her conversation with Professor Strauss, adding Amelia's frantic journal entries. Dr. Schmidt listened intently, his expression growing grave.

"During the Nazi occupation," he explained, "there were networks of resistance fighters who helped artists and intellectuals escape persecution. These networks often used coded messages hidden in music or literature."

A spark of hope ignited within Elena. "So, these notes could be a message from a Jewish composer Amelia was helping?"

Dr. Schmidt nodded cautiously. "It's certainly a possibility. Deciphering the code, however, would be a daunting task. We'd need someone familiar with pre-war musical codes and the resistance movement."

He suggested contacting Herr Wagner, a retired codebreaker who specialized in wartime ciphers.

Living in a quiet suburb on the outskirts of Vienna, Herr Wagner was a gruff man shrouded in an aura of quiet sadness.

He listened to Elena's story with a weary nod, his gaze fixed on the faded sheet music.

"These notes are clever," he muttered, his voice a low rumble. "They incorporate elements of musical notation, but also esoteric symbols used by resistance groups in Vienna during the war."

A FLICKER OF EXCITEMENT lit his eyes.

"Cracking this code will take time, but I believe it's possible. It could be a piece of forgotten history, a message waiting to be heard."

As Elena left Herr Wagner's house, the weight of the violin case in her hand felt heavier, but now it held a promise – the promise of unearthing a hidden story, a melody silenced by war, waiting to be played once again.

The city of Vienna, with its contrasting beauty and buried secrets, had become not just a destination, but a portal to the past, a past she was determined to understand.

Chapter 5: Echoes in the City of Music

Vienna unfolded its secrets slowly, like a reluctant lover revealing a hidden past. Elena spent her days navigating the labyrinthine streets, a map clutched in one hand and Amelia's journal in the other.

She visited the imposing Hofburg Palace, once the seat of the Habsburg dynasty, now a silent witness to the city's tumultuous history.

She stood on the steps of the Vienna State Opera, the grand facade a stark contrast to the chilling stories of artists banned from its hallowed stage.

Everywhere she went, the city whispered of Amelia's life. She imagined the young violinist walking these same streets, her violin case a shield against the growing darkness.

Elena visited bustling cafes, where musicians once filled the air with their melodies, and now tourists sipped their cappuccinos, oblivious to the ghosts of the past.

The evenings were spent in Dr. Schmidt's office, pouring over dusty archives and historical documents.

They discovered snippets of information – a mention of a Jewish composer named David Berger who vanished during the war, a reference to a hidden network called the "Harmonie Society" that helped artists escape persecution.

Each piece, though small, fueled Elena's determination.

One afternoon, while scouring a local newspaper archive, Elena found a faded photograph tucked within the brittle pages. It depicted a concert hall, filled with an enthusiastic audience.

In the center, violin held high, stood Amelia, a radiant smile illuminating her face. But beside her, barely visible in the grainy photograph, stood a young man with a shock of dark hair and a hint of defiance in his eyes.

The caption below confirmed Elena's suspicions – "Amelia Hartmann and rising composer David Berger perform to a sold-out crowd."

Her heart pounded in her chest. This was David, the composer Amelia mentioned in her cryptic notes.

The pieces were starting to fall into place. Dr. Schmidt shared Elena's excitement. "David Berger's disappearance is a documented tragedy," he said, his voice tinged with sadness. "His music was deemed degenerate because of his heritage.

This could be the missing key, a hidden message he entrusted to Amelia."

Meanwhile, Herr Wagner, the retired codebreaker, worked tirelessly on deciphering the musical score.

He meticulously compared the notes to known resistance symbols and musical codes, his days filled with silence broken only by the scribblings of his pen and the occasional frustrated mutter.

One evening, as Elena sat in her small hotel room, Amelia's journal clutched in her hand, a sense of loneliness washed over her.

She felt an inexplicable bond with this woman from the past, a woman who shared her love for music and faced an unimaginable darkness.

Picking up the violin, Elena felt its cool wood against her fingertips.

Tentatively, she drew the bow across the strings.

A single, piercing note echoed through the room, a mournful sound that resonated with the city's unspoken history.

Elena closed her eyes, and in the silence that followed, she could almost hear a melody – a melody of loss, of defiance, and of a love story silenced by war.

The city of music was filled with echoes, and Elena knew she had only just begun to listen.

Chapter 6: A Prodigy's Dream

Vienna, 1938. Spring painted the city in a burst of vibrant colors.

Young Amelia Hartmann, barely eighteen, practiced her violin with a fervor that bordered on obsession.

Sunlight streamed through the ornate windows of her music studio, illuminating dust motes dancing in the golden rays.

The room, with its well-worn Persian rug and mahogany furniture, held the echoes of countless hours dedicated to mastering her craft.

Today, however, a tremor of nervousness ran through Amelia's hands.

Tomorrow was the annual Vienna Philharmonic competition, the pinnacle of achievement for any aspiring musician in Austria.

The judges were renowned for their strictness, and the competition fierce.

But Amelia was determined.

Music wasn't just a passion; it was her very essence.

Since childhood, she'd held a violin in her hands, its familiar curves like an extension of her body.

Melodies flowed through her like the Danube River, a constant current of emotions yearning to be expressed.

Music was her sanctuary, a language transcending words, a way to capture the beauty and complexity of the world around her.

A knock on the door shattered her concentration. In walked her mother, Frau Hartmann, a woman whose gentle demeanor belied a steely core.

Her eyes, usually filled with warmth, held a flicker of worry. "Amelia, darling," she said as she entered, the air around her heavy with unspoken concerns. "Have you eaten?"

Amelia glanced at the overturned bowl of cereal on the coffee table, a testament to her single-minded focus. "Not yet, Mama," she admitted sheepishly.

Frau Hartmann chuckled softly.

"Come, take a break. Your stomach needs fuel just as much as your talent."

She led Amelia to the balcony overlooking a bustling street.

Below, the city thrummed with activity, a symphony of honking cars, street vendors hawking their wares, and the distant laughter of children.

There was a tense silence between them. Amelia knew her mother worried about the changing political climate.

Nazi rhetoric had become increasingly belligerent, anti-Semitic propaganda poisoning the airwaves.

Amelia's best friend, a gifted young pianist named Sarah Bernstein, had already left for Switzerland with her family, a chilling reminder of the growing fear.

"Are you scared, Amelia?" her mother finally asked, her voice barely a whisper.

Amelia met her mother's gaze, a steely resolve hardening her features.

"I might be nervous about the competition," she said, "but I won't let fear stop me from playing. Music has the power to unite, to uplift, to speak truth in times of darkness."

Frau Hartmann offered a wan smile. "You have such a pure heart, Amelia. Never lose sight of that."

She reached out and squeezed Amelia's hand.

"Now, finish your breakfast and show those judges what you're made of. Vienna needs music like yours now more than ever."

Emboldened by her mother's words, Amelia returned to her practice session. The sun dipped below the horizon, painting the sky in fiery hues.

As the melody poured from her violin, clear and unwavering, Amelia knew this was more than just a performance; it was a declaration of passion, a defiant cry for hope in the face of uncertainty.

Chapter 7: Whispers of Change

The year 1938 cast a long shadow over Vienna.

The once vibrant city seemed to hold its breath, a collective unease simmering beneath the surface.

Swastika flags fluttered from balconies, replacing the cheerful flower boxes that used to brighten the streets.

Book burnings filled the air with the acrid scent of burning paper, a chilling reminder of the suppression of art deemed "degenerate."

Amelia, despite her youthful optimism, couldn't ignore the changes. Fear hung heavy in the air, especially amongst her Jewish friends.

Sarah's absence left a gaping hole in her life, their shared dreams of performing on the world stage replaced by a gnawing anxiety.

One evening, at a local cafe frequented by artists and intellectuals, Amelia bumped into David Berger, a young composer with a mop of dark hair and eyes that sparkled with a mischievous glint.

Their friendship had blossomed over shared late-night practice sessions and passionate discussions about music.

David, unlike Amelia, openly voiced his anger at the rising tide of fascism.

"They want to control our minds, Amelia," he said, his voice low and urgent, as they sat tucked away in a corner booth.

"They want to dictate what art is, what music is allowed to be heard. It's an act of barbarism."

Amelia nodded, her heart heavy.

She'd seen some of David's compositions – bold, innovative pieces that defied traditional structures. They were beautiful and raw, a reflection of the turmoil within him.

"We can't let them silence us," David continued, his voice gaining defiance. "Our music is a weapon, a way to fight back. A way to keep hope alive."

Those words ignited a spark within Amelia.

She, too, felt a responsibility to use her music as a form of resistance, a beacon of light in the encroaching darkness.

They started collaborating, intertwining their talents to create pieces that spoke of love, loss, and the unwavering human spirit.

One afternoon, while rummaging through a dusty music shop, Amelia stumbled upon a collection of banned music.

The sheet music, filled with avant-garde notation and cryptic symbols, felt like a forbidden language, a hidden message yearning to be understood.

Intrigued, she bought the collection, a rebellious act in a city where such defiance could have consequences.

Back at her apartment, David examined the sheet music with a mixture of fascination and trepidation.

"These are the works of composers blacklisted by the regime," he whispered, tracing the unfamiliar symbols with his finger. "They're coded, a way to express dissent without drawing attention."

A thrill shot through Amelia.

This was a secret society of musicians, using their art as a form of rebellion.

Suddenly, their own compositions held more meaning – a defiance whispered through notes, a message hidden in plain sight.

The act of playing their music, even in private, became a shared act of resistance, a small victory in the face of oppression.

As the months passed, the city tightened its grip.

Anti-Semitic laws became more stringent, fear becoming a constant companion.

But Amelia and David clung to their music, their secret language a shield against the encroaching darkness.

They knew a storm was brewing, but they were determined to face it together, their music a defiant melody in the face of a world teetering on the brink.

Chapter 8: Forbidden Notes

The air crackled with tension as Amelia and David huddled in her dimly lit apartment.

Rain lashed against the windows, a rhythmic counterpoint to the nervous tapping of David's foot.

He held a worn leather satchel in his lap, its contents weighing heavily on him.

"This is it, Amelia," he said, his voice barely a whisper.

"This is my life's work, everything I've composed."

He gestured towards the satchel. "I can't risk keeping it here."

Amelia's heart ached for David.

The fear in his eyes mirrored her own.

The Nazi regime had intensified its persecution of Jews, and David, a rising star in the city's music scene, was now a target.

"We need to get it out of Austria," she said, her voice firm despite the tremor in her hands. "But how?"

David unfolded a map, its creases worn from countless nights spent planning.

"There's an underground network, the 'Harmonie Society.' They help artists and intellectuals escape persecution and smuggle their work out of the country."

A flicker of hope ignited within Amelia.

The Harmonie Society was a whispered legend among artists, a lifeline for those threatened by the regime.

"Do you have a contact?" she asked.

David nodded, his gaze flicking to a small photograph tucked into the map.

It depicted a woman with kind eyes and a smile etched by years of experience.

"Her name is Frau Schmidt. She's one of their leaders."

The following night, Amelia found herself in a nondescript building on the outskirts of the city.

A nervous knot twisted in her stomach as she knocked on the weathered door.

A moment later, it creaked open, revealing Frau Schmidt, her face etched with concern.

David, his face pale under the dim light, explained his situation.

Frau Schmidt listened intently, her eyes reflecting the weight of the task ahead.

"Smuggling art is a dangerous business," she said, her voice a low rasp.

"But we will do everything in our power to help."

She explained the plan.

David's music would be hidden within a seemingly ordinary violin case, a secret compartment meticulously crafted by a skilled woodcarver who sympathized with the cause. Amelia, posing as David's traveling companion, would accompany the music across the border.

A bittersweet farewell unfolded in Amelia's apartment. The weight of the unknown hung heavy in the air.

David, his eyes filled with gratitude, handed Amelia the violin case.

"Take care of her, Amelia," he whispered, his voice thick with emotion.

"Take care of my music."

Tears welled up in Amelia's eyes, but she held them back.

She knew this wasn't goodbye, but rather a pause in their melody, a promise to reunite when the world was less cruel.

As dawn painted the sky with streaks of orange and pink, Amelia boarded the train, the violin case clutched tightly in her trembling hands.

She carried not just an instrument, but a legacy of defiance, a symphony of hope smuggled across a border, a melody yearning to be played on the other side.

Chapter 9: A Dangerous Secret

The train rattled and groaned as it snaked its way through the Austrian countryside.

Amelia gripped the violin case, its worn leather a source of comfort amidst the swirling anxieties churning in her stomach.

Every creak of the wheels, every glance from a fellow passenger, fueled her fear of discovery.

Frau Schmidt had warned her of the dangers. Nazi patrols were frequent, searching for contraband or anyone attempting to flee the country.

Amelia had practiced her cover story – a student traveling to Switzerland to visit a sick aunt. But with each passing minute, the weight of responsibility became a crushing burden.

The border crossing was the most nerve-wracking part.

Passengers were herded out of the train, lugging their bags towards a long queue.

Amelia clutched the violin case closer, her heart hammering against her ribs.

As she inched forward, the barking of a German Shepherd and the gruff voices of border guards intensified her panic.

A uniformed officer, his face a mask of stoicism, inspected her passport.

He cast a suspicious glance at the violin case.

"What's in here?" he barked, his voice thick with a foreign accent.

Amelia felt her knees weaken.

She willed her voice to remain steady as she replied, "Just a violin, sir. I'm a music student."

The officer grunted, his hand hovering over the latches.

The seconds stretched into an eternity until, finally, he waved her through.

Relief washed over Amelia, so powerful it almost brought tears to her eyes. She had cleared the first hurdle, but her journey was far from over.

Switzerland loomed on the horizon, a haven for those fleeing persecution.

But reaching it meant navigating a treacherous mountain pass, a route favored by smugglers and refugees alike.

Frau Schmidt had provided her with a map and a contact – a gruff mountain guide named Franz who knew the terrain like the back of his hand.

Franz, a weathered man with a stoic demeanor, awaited them at a small, deserted train station nestled in a valley.

He eyed Amelia with a mix of skepticism and grudging respect.

"You sure you're up for this, Fräulein?" he rasped, his voice as rough as the mountains he traversed.

Amelia squared her shoulders.

"I have to be," she said, her voice firm despite her trembling hands.

"This violin case carries more than just an instrument."

Franz grunted in understanding.

He led them to a small, hidden path that snaked up a sheer mountain face.

The air grew thin and crisp, the only sounds the crunch of their boots on gravel and the distant cry of eagles circling overhead.

Hours melted into a blur of exhaustion and exhilaration.

Amelia pushed herself further than she thought possible, fueled by the weight of her mission.

Finally, after a grueling climb, they reached the crest of the mountain.

Switzerland, a land of rolling green hills and sparkling lakes, stretched out before them like a promise of freedom.

Amelia sank to her knees, tears blurring her vision.

They had made it. David's music, a testament to defiance, was safe on foreign soil, a song waiting to be heard.

As they descended the mountain on the Swiss side, Franz stopped at a secluded clearing.

A lone figure emerged from the trees – an elderly woman with eyes that held a lifetime of stories.

Frau Schmidt's relief mirrored Amelia's. "You made it," she said, her voice thick with emotion. "The music is safe now."

Amelia handed the violin case to Frau Schmidt, a weight lifting from her shoulders.

She had played her part, a small note in a grand symphony of resistance.

As they said their goodbyes, Amelia knew she might never see these brave people again.

But their courage, their willingness to stand against oppression, would forever be etched in her memory.

Chapter 10: Love in the Time of War

Returning to Vienna felt like stepping back into a nightmare. The city, once vibrant and alive, now seemed shrouded in a suffocating silence.

Swastika flags flaunted their menacing dominance, and fear hung heavy in the air.

Amelia, burdened by her secret and the guilt of leaving David behind, struggled to find solace in the familiar surroundings.

Days turned into weeks, each one marked by a growing sense of isolation.

She kept the violin case hidden, the secret compartment a constant reminder of her responsibility.

She desperately wanted to play David's music, to hear his defiance resonate within the confines of her apartment walls.

But the risk was too great.

One afternoon, while browsing through a dusty bookstore, Amelia stumbled upon a hidden gem – a small, clandestine music club tucked away in a basement.

A faded poster advertised an evening of "underground music."

Hope flared within her.

This could be a haven, a space where music transcended politics, where dissent flickered like a candle in the darkness.

That night, Amelia ventured into the dimly lit basement.

A small crowd of people, a mix of ages and backgrounds, huddled around a makeshift stage.

The air crackled with nervous excitement.

As the night unfolded, musicians took turns performing works that whispered defiance – coded messages hidden within melodies, sorrowful cries disguised as waltzes.

Amelia felt a wave of emotion wash over her.

These were her people, the keepers of a forbidden language, fighting back with the only weapon they had – their art.

After the last performance, a hush fell over the room.

Amelia, her heart pounding in her chest, approached the organizer, a man with a worn face and eyes filled with defiance.

"I have something I need to play," she said, her voice barely a whisper.

He studied her for a moment, his gaze assessing.

"Let me hear it," he finally said, a hint of curiosity flickering in his eyes.

Taking a deep breath, Amelia retrieved the violin from its case.

Her fingers trembled as they touched the familiar strings.

Then, she began to play.

David's music soared through the air, a vibrant tapestry of notes filled with anger, love, and a desperate yearning for freedom.

The room held its breath, captivated by the raw emotion pouring from the violin.

When the last note faded, a stunned silence hung in the air.

Then, a single clap broke the spell, followed by another, and another.

Tears welled up in Amelia's eyes, not just tears of relief, but tears of unity.

They were not alone in their defiance.

In this hidden space, music had become a weapon, a symphony of resistance echoing through the darkness.

As Amelia left the club that night, clutching the violin close, she knew the fight was far from over.

But tonight, the air felt just a little lighter, the city a little less oppressive.

David's music, a testament to their shared defiance, had found its voice, a beacon of hope in the midst of a brewing storm.

The melody, whispered through the notes, would continue to resonate, a message carried across time, waiting for the day it could be played in the light.

Chapter 11: A City Transformed

———

Years bled into decades, the Second World War leaving its indelible scars on the face of Europe.

Vienna, once a vibrant city of music and art, emerged from the ashes a changed place.

The grand buildings bore the marks of conflict, their scars a constant reminder of the darkness that had passed.

Elena, her hair now streaked with silver, stood on the steps of the Vienna State Opera.

The once-silenced stage was now alive with bustling activity, musicians practicing for the upcoming season.

A sense of peace, fragile yet undeniable, settled in her heart.

Holding Amelia's journal in her hand, she remembered the young woman who had defied a regime with her music, the woman who had entrusted her with a secret symphony.

Elena's journey had brought her full circle, from a dusty attic to the heart of Vienna's artistic renaissance.

Professor Strauss, his frail form now strengthened by the passage of time, greeted her with a warm smile.

"You look well, Elena," he said, his voice raspy but kind.

"Herr Wagner, bless his stubborn soul, finally cracked the code."

Elena's heart skipped a beat.

"He did? David Berger's music, we can finally hear it?"

Professor Strauss nodded, his eyes twinkling with anticipation.

"Indeed. He's transcribed the notes into traditional notation, a testament to a silenced voice. The Vienna Philharmonic has agreed to perform it as part of their upcoming season."

The news filled Elena with a mix of excitement and trepidation.

David's music, a message from a bygone era, was ready to be heard by a new generation.

Would it resonate?

Would it spark a conversation about the past, a past that should never be forgotten?

The night of the concert arrived, the air buzzing with anticipation.

Elena sat in the front row, the worn violin case resting on her lap, a silent companion on this momentous occasion.

As the orchestra took its place, a hush fell over the audience.

The conductor raised his baton, and the first notes of David Berger's composition filled the hall.

The music was unlike anything Elena had ever heard.

It was a torrent of emotions – anger, defiance, hope, and a profound sense of loss.

It painted a picture of a city on the brink, of artists forced into hiding, of love threatened by oppression.

It was a lament for the past, but also a celebration of the human spirit's ability to endure.

Tears streamed down Elena's cheeks as the final note faded away.

The audience erupted in thunderous applause, a wave of appreciation washing over the concert hall.

Elena knew, in that moment, that David's music had transcended time.

It was a reminder of the power of art to inspire, to unite, and to keep the flame of hope burning even in the darkest of times.

Later that evening, Elena stood before Amelia's grave, the city lights twinkling in the distance.

She placed the violin case gently on the headstone.

"They played your friend's music tonight, Amelia," she whispered, her voice thick with emotion.

"The city remembers."

As the moon cast a silver glow over the cemetery, Elena felt a sense of closure.

Amelia's story, once hidden in an attic trunk, had been brought to light.

The melody, whispered through notes and carried across decades, had finally found its voice, a testament to the enduring power of music and the courage of those who dared to defy silence.

Chapter 12: A Legacy Reborn

———

Years had passed since the concert, but the memory of David Berger's music lingered in Vienna's cultural consciousness.

It became a touchstone, a reminder of the city's tumultuous past and the enduring power of artistic expression.

Elena, now a respected music historian, found herself frequently giving talks about Amelia and David, their story resonating with a new generation.

One afternoon, a young violinist named Clara approached Elena after a lecture.

Clara, with fiery red hair and a passionate gaze, confessed she'd been deeply moved by David's music.

She was preparing for a competition and felt an inexplicable connection to his compositions.

"There's something raw and powerful about his work," Clara explained, her voice filled with admiration. "It feels like a story waiting to be told."

Elena felt a spark ignite within her.

Perhaps David's message wasn't meant to be a relic of the past.

Maybe it held the power to inspire a new generation of artists.

She shared Amelia's journal and the original sheet music with Clara, igniting a collaborative spirit.

Clara spent weeks immersing herself in David's work, meticulously studying his notes and the hidden messages embedded within.

She saw a reflection of Amelia's courage and David's defiance, their love story woven into the very fabric of the music.

As Clara practiced, Elena saw a flicker of Amelia's spirit in the young woman's fiery passion.

Together, they decided to create a new performance piece.

They incorporated elements of traditional music with David's innovative composition, creating a moving narrative that intertwined love, loss, and the fight for freedom.

The violin case, a silent witness to the past, became a symbol of resilience, passed from Amelia to Clara as a conduit for their shared legacy.

The day of the competition arrived, and the concert hall hummed with anticipation. Clara, nervousness tinged with determination, walked onto the stage.

As she raised her violin and drew the bow across the strings, the hall fell silent.

The music soared, a testament to a love story silenced by war, a defiant cry for hope, and a celebration of the human spirit's ability to overcome adversity.

Clara's performance was electrifying.

The audience, captivated by the raw emotion pouring from the violin, erupted in thunderous applause.

Tears welled up in Elena's eyes, not just for the sheer brilliance of the performance, but for the legacy it carried.

David's music, once a whisper in the darkness, had become a powerful roar, a message echoing across generations, reminding everyone of the importance of fighting for what one believes in, and the enduring power of love and art in a world that desperately needs it.

As Clara bowed, a single spotlight illuminated the violin case resting on a stand beside her.

It was a simple wooden case, yet it held within it a lifetime of stories, a testament to the enduring power of music, and a promise that the melody, once silenced, would continue to resonate, inspiring future generations to raise their voices and create their own symphonies of hope.

Chapter 13: Echoes in a New World

News of Clara's performance spread like wildfire.

Videos of her electrifying rendition of David Berger's music garnered millions of views online.

The story behind the music, meticulously researched by Elena, captivated audiences worldwide.

A forgotten composer, a love story lost to history, and a violin case holding a legacy – it resonated with people yearning for connection and meaning in a world increasingly dominated by technology and division.

Invitations poured in.

Clara, thrust into the international spotlight, found herself performing at prestigious concert halls around the globe.

From Carnegie Hall to the Sydney Opera House, David's music, infused with Clara's passionate interpretation, resonated with audiences from all walks of life.

Elena, ever the historian, accompanied Clara on these journeys, sharing Amelia and David's story at pre-concert talks.

She witnessed the impact of their music firsthand – tears streaming down faces, standing ovations, and heartfelt conversations sparked by the forgotten melodies.

David's message, a cry for freedom from a bygone era, seemed more relevant than ever.

One evening, after a performance in Berlin, a frail woman approached Elena backstage.

Her eyes, clouded by age but filled with spark, held a familiar glint.

"You must be Elena," she said, her voice raspy but resolute. "I knew Amelia. We were friends in school."

A wave of emotion washed over Elena.

This woman, a living connection to Amelia, a piece of the past she thought lost forever.

They spent hours talking, sharing memories and filling in the gaps of Amelia's story.

The woman revealed Amelia's talent for painting, a hidden passion she nurtured alongside her music.

Intrigued, Elena started digging deeper.

Hidden away in a dusty attic, she discovered a collection of Amelia's paintings – vibrant landscapes, portraits filled with emotion, and one, a haunting depiction of a violinist playing a forbidden melody in a dimly lit room.

The image mirrored Clara's performance so perfectly it sent chills down Elena's spine.

Inspired, Elena decided to curate an exhibit.

She combined Amelia's paintings with David's recovered sheet music and Clara's performance footage. T

he exhibit, titled "Echoes from the Silence," became a sensation.

Visitors from all walks of life marveled at the beauty of Amelia's paintings, felt the raw emotion of David's music, and were captivated by Clara's performance.

"Echoes from the Silence" transcended a mere artistic showcase.

It became a conversation starter, reminding people of the perils of silence, the importance of artistic expression, and the enduring power of love and defiance in the face of oppression.

The exhibit traveled the world, a testament to the interconnectedness of human experience, and a powerful symbol of how art transcends borders, languages, and time.

Years later, on the anniversary of Amelia's birth,

Elena stood at her grave, a bouquet of wildflowers in hand.

The melody of David's music, faint yet clear, seemed to linger in the air.

Smiling to herself, Elena whispered, "You see, Amelia, your story is not forgotten.

Your music, like your paintings, continues to inspire."

The legacy of the violin case, once a silent witness to a hidden story, had blossomed into a powerful force, a testament to the enduring power of art.

The melody, whispered through notes and carried across generations, had become a symphony of hope, reminding the world of the importance of fighting for what one believes in, and the transformative power of music and art to connect us all.

Chapter 14: A Distant Harmony

News of "Echoes from the Silence" reached a small village nestled amidst the snow-capped peaks of the Swiss Alps.

An elderly woman, her face lined with the stories of a long life, sat by a crackling fireplace, a newspaper clipping clutched in her wrinkled hands.

The faded photograph depicted Clara, mid-performance, her violin case emblazoned with a single, worn sunflower.

Frau Schmidt, her eyes welling with tears, recognized the case instantly.

It was the very same one she had entrusted to Amelia all those years ago.

A wave of memories flooded back – the fear etched on Amelia's face, the weight of responsibility, the quiet hope for a future where David's music could be heard.

The newspaper proclaimed Clara as a rising star, David Berger's compositions hailed as a powerful rediscovery.

A pang of regret pierced Frau Schmidt's heart.

She never saw David again, never knew if he managed to escape the clutches of the regime.

But seeing his music reach a new generation, stirring emotions and sparking conversations, brought a bittersweet comfort.

Fueled by a newfound purpose, Frau Schmidt dug through a dusty trunk hidden in the back of her attic.

Yellowed letters, tied with a faded ribbon, revealed a long-forgotten correspondence between David and a young pianist named Sarah Bernstein.

The letters spoke of a budding friendship, shared dreams of performing on the world stage, and a heartbreaking farewell as Sarah and her family fled to America.

A spark ignited within Frau Schmidt.

Perhaps, just perhaps, Sarah was still alive.

With trembling hands, she reached out to a network of friends who had helped artists escape during the war.

Days turned into weeks, filled with anticipation and gnawing uncertainty. Then, a glimmer of hope.

A woman named Sarah Miller resided in a quiet town on the outskirts of New York City.

Frau Schmidt penned a letter, pouring her heart out, recounting the story of David's music, and the young violinist who had brought it back to life.

Weeks later, a reply arrived, the elegant script a mirror of Sarah's youthful handwriting. Tears streamed down Frau Schmidt's face as she read Sarah's response, a heartfelt confirmation of her identity.

The letter spoke of a life built anew, a successful career as a concert pianist, and a heart forever marked by loss.

But most importantly, it expressed a profound gratitude for David's music being played once more, a testament to the love story silenced by war.

Frau Schmidt knew what she had to do.

Months later, a frail woman with eyes twinkling with a lifetime of stories stood backstage at Carnegie Hall.

Sarah Bernstein, her hair now silver but her spirit undimmed, gazed at Clara with awe.

As the final note of David's composition faded, a standing ovation erupted, the echoes resonating through the grand hall.

Tears welled up in Sarah's eyes.

This wasn't just a performance; it was a reunion, a bridge across time and continents.

David's music, imbued with their shared past, had brought them together, a melody of love and loss that transcended borders and defied the years.

In that moment, surrounded by the power of music and the warmth of human connection, Sarah knew David's legacy lived on.

The melody whispered through notes, carried across generations, had finally found a chorus, a global symphony of hope, a testament to the enduring power of art to heal, unite, and remind us that even in the darkest of times, the echoes of love and defiance can never truly be silenced.

Chapter 15: A New Dawn

The world had transformed since Amelia's time.

Technology had woven its way into every aspect of life, information flowing at the speed of light.

Yet, amidst the digital buzz, the melody from the violin case continued to resonate.

A young filmmaker named Leo, captivated by "Echoes from the Silence," embarked on a project of his own.

Leo, driven by a desire to breathe new life into Amelia and David's story, envisioned a documentary film.

He meticulously researched their lives, interviewing Clara, Elena, and even Sarah, who shared her memories of David with a bittersweet ache.

He delved into historical archives, unearthing grainy footage of pre-war Vienna, the city pulsating with music and life before the darkness descended.

The film, titled "The Unfinished Symphony," interweaved interviews, historical footage, and animated sequences that brought Amelia and David's love story to life.

David's music, masterfully reinterpreted by Clara, served as the film's emotional core, each note echoing their struggles, their love, and their unwavering spirit.

The premiere of "The Unfinished Symphony" at the Vienna International Film Festival was a momentous occasion.

Survivors of the war, their faces etched with the weight of the past, sat alongside a new generation eager to learn about this forgotten chapter in history.

As the credits rolled, a hush fell over the auditorium, followed by a wave of applause that seemed to shake the very foundations of the building.

The film resonated globally.

Streamed on countless platforms, it sparked conversations about the dangers of silencing dissent, the importance of artistic expression, and the enduring power of love in the face of oppression.

Schools incorporated it into their curriculums, prompting discussions about tolerance and the fight for human rights.

One evening, after a screening at a local university, Leo was approached by a young woman named Maya.

Her eyes, filled with curiosity, mirrored Amelia's youthful passion.

"What happened to David?" she asked, her voice barely a whisper.

Leo smiled sadly.

"We don't know for sure, Maya. He likely perished during the war."

A heavy silence descended upon them.

"But his music lives on," Maya continued, her voice filled with determinatio

"And Amelia's story. It reminds us that we can't let fear silence us."

Leo's heart swelled with a sense of hope.

Amelia and David's story, once confined to a dusty attic and a worn violin case, had become a global conversation starter, a testament to the enduring power of art to inspire future generations.

The melody, whispered through notes and carried across decades, had become a symphony of defiance, a reminder that even the smallest act of courage can leave a lasting echo, a call to action for a world yearning for understanding and unity.

As Maya walked away, a flicker of Amelia's spirit seemed to linger in the air, a promise that the music, and the fight for what one believes in, would continue to inspire long into the future.

Chapter 16: A Legacy Carries On

Years flowed by, etching new stories onto the tapestry of time.

The melody from the violin case, however, remained a constant thread, woven into the fabric of countless lives.

One sunny afternoon, in a bustling music shop nestled on a quiet Parisian street, a young violinist named Elise browsed the rows of instruments.

Elise, with her fiery red hair and a gaze that mirrored Clara's intensity, possessed a raw talent that captivated her teachers.

But a nagging doubt gnawed at her – a sense that her music lacked a deeper purpose.

As she ran her fingers across the smooth surface of a violin, her eyes caught a glint of gold tucked away in a corner display.

It was a worn violin case, a single, faded sunflower emblazoned on its side.

Intrigued, Elise approached the shopkeeper, a kind-faced woman with eyes that held a lifetime of stories.

"That case," Elise inquired, her voice filled with curiosity, "is there a story behind it?"

The shopkeeper's smile widened.

"Ah, that case," she said, her voice a gentle rasp.

"It belonged to a young woman named Amelia, a brave soul who fought for music's freedom during a dark time."

Over steaming cups of tea, the shopkeeper, her name was Madame Rousseau, recounted the story of Amelia, David, and the secret symphony nestled within the case.

Elise listened, captivated, as the past unfolded before her, the struggles and triumphs resonating deeply within her.

"The music inside," Madame Rousseau continued, her voice dropping to a reverent whisper, "it's a testament to the enduring power of love and art.

It's waiting for the right person to play it again."

Elise felt a tremor of excitement course through her.

Could she be that person? With trembling hands, she opened the case.

Inside, nestled in velvet lining, lay a violin, its wood bearing the marks of time, yet emanating a quiet power.

As Elise drew the bow across the strings, the melody unfolded, a bittersweet symphony of defiance and hope.

The shop filled with the music, captivating customers and passersby alike.

Madame Rousseau, tears welling in her eyes, felt a connection to a bygone era, a sense that Amelia's legacy was being carried forward.

When the last note faded, a stunned silence hung in the air, followed by a slow, appreciative applause.

Elise knew, in that moment, her purpose.

She wouldn't just play David's music; she would carry on its legacy.

She would use it to inspire others, to fight for artistic freedom, and to remind the world of the importance of love and courage in the face of adversity.

Word of Elise's performance spread quickly.

Soon, she was invited to perform at prestigious venues, sharing not just the music, but the story behind it.

The violin case, once a silent witness to a hidden past, became a symbol of hope, a testament to the ongoing struggle for free expression.

One evening, after a performance at a music festival, a group of young musicians approached Elise.

Their eyes shone with a shared passion, a desire to make a difference through their art.

"We want to learn more," one of them said, his voice filled with determination.

"We want to be part of something bigger than ourselves."

Elise smiled, a warmth spreading through her.

She wasn't alone.

The melody, whispered through notes and carried across decades, had become a rallying cry.

It had united a new generation of artists, their voices blending into a powerful chorus, a symphony of defiance that echoed across the globe.

As she looked out at the sea of faces, young and old, diverse and united by their love for music, Elise knew this was just the beginning.

The legacy of the violin case, a simple object that held a universe of stories, would continue to inspire, reminding everyone that even the smallest act of courage can leave a lasting echo, and that the melody of hope, once set free, will forever resonate, inspiring future generations to raise their voices and create their own symphonies of change.

Chapter 17: Echoes in the Digital Age

The year is 2047.

The world is a tapestry woven with gleaming skyscrapers and sprawling virtual landscapes.

Technology reigns supreme, information accessible at the tap of a finger, and music a constant companion, pulsing through earbuds and AI-generated playlists.

Yet, amidst the digital hum, the melody from the violin case continues its quiet revolution.

Elise, her fiery hair now touched with silver, stood before a throng of virtual avatars, their holographic forms hovering in a vast online auditorium.

No longer a young prodigy, she was a revered conductor, a living bridge between the past and the digital future.

Tonight, she was leading a global orchestra, a real-world ensemble blended with their virtual counterparts, in a performance dedicated to the legacy of David Berger.

The concert was a groundbreaking event, streamed live across the globe.

Millions watched, captivated by the synergy between the human musicians and their AI counterparts.

As Elise raised her baton, the familiar melody soared, traversing continents and defying the limitations of the physical world.

The performance wasn't just about music.

It was a call to action.

Elise, in between movements, shared Amelia's story, the fight for artistic freedom, and the importance of preserving the past in a world obsessed with the future.

The audience, a diverse mix of ages and cultures, engaged in real-time discussions, their avatars sparking conversations about censorship, the rise of AI in creative fields, and the enduring power of human stories.

After the final note faded, the virtual applause seemed to reverberate across the real world.

Elise, overwhelmed with emotion, addressed the audience.

"This music," she said, her voice filled with conviction, "is a reminder that even in the digital age, the human spirit craves connection and expression.

Let it inspire you to raise your voices, to fight for what you believe in, and to create your own symphonies of change."

The impact of the concert was far-reaching.

A wave of citizen-created remixes and reinterpretations of David's music flooded the internet.

Artists, inspired by Elise's message, began incorporating historical narratives into their virtual creations.

Museums and educational institutions launched immersive experiences that brought Amelia and David's story to life.

One day, Elise received a message from a young programmer named Kai.

A prodigy in the field of AI music generation, Kai had been deeply moved by the concert.

He proposed a collaboration – using AI to complete David's unfinished symphony, based on the existing notes and the emotional context of his life.

Elise was initially skeptical.

Could AI truly capture the essence of human emotion?

But after witnessing Kai's passion and the sophistication of his algorithms, she agreed.

The collaboration was a challenging yet rewarding process.

Kai's AI helped bridge the gaps in the composition, while Elise meticulously ensured that the newly created sections retained David's spirit.

The premiere of the completed symphony was a monumental event.

The performance, a blend of traditional instruments and AI-generated soundscapes, transported the audience to a bygone era while simultaneously pushing the boundaries of music itself.

Tears streamed down Elise's face as the final note echoed through the concert hall.

David's silenced voice, now complete, resonated with a newfound power, a testament to the enduring legacy of human creativity and the transformative potential of technology used for good.

As the world continued to evolve, the melody from the violin case remained a constant thread, a reminder that the fight for freedom and the power of art are timeless struggles.

In the ever-evolving landscape of music and technology, the symphony of defiance continued to play, an echo carried across time, a testament to the enduring power of a single violin case and the stories it held within.

Chapter 18: A Legacy Forged in Unity

DECADES HAD PASSED since the groundbreaking performance of David Berger's completed symphony.

The world had undergone a dramatic shift.

Climate change had reshaped landscapes, forcing humanity to adapt and collaborate on a global scale.

Virtual reality experiences became commonplace, blurring the lines between the physical and digital worlds.

Yet, the melody from the violin case continued to resonate, a powerful symbol of unity and resilience.

Elise, a revered elder stateswoman in the music world, lived in a self-sustaining community nestled amongst the ruins of a once-great city.

Here, amidst the remnants of the past, a new society thrived on shared resources and a deep appreciation for history.

One crisp morning, a young woman named Anya, her eyes brimming with curiosity, approached Elise.

"Tell me again about the violin case," Anya pleaded, her voice tinged with a youthful yearning for connection.

Elise smiled, the wrinkles on her face deepening as countless stories flickered behind her eyes.

Settling into a weathered armchair, she began to weave the familiar tale – Amelia's courage, David's defiance, the music that defied silence.

As Anya listened, a sense of awe settled upon her.

These events, though distant in time, resonated deeply with the struggles her own generation faced – the fight for environmental sustainability and the ever-present threat of social control through virtual realities.

"The music," Elise concluded, her voice husky with emotion, "became a bridge, connecting the past to the present.

It reminded us of the power of art to inspire change."

Anya's brow furrowed.

"But how can music change anything in a world like ours?" she questioned, her voice reflecting the disillusionment of her generation.

Elise chuckled, a warm, knowing sound.

"Music," she explained, "has the power to speak to the soul, to evoke emotions that transcend words. It can unite us in our shared humanity, reminding us of what truly matters – love, hope, and the courage to fight for a better future."

Inspired by Elise's words, Anya embarked on a mission.

Utilizing her skills in virtual reality design, she began creating an immersive experience based on Amelia and David's story.

Working tirelessly, she weaved historical facts with artistic license, transporting users to the heart of pre-war Vienna, allowing them to experience the city's vibrant music scene and the stifling oppression that followed.

The VR experience, titled "Echoes of Defiance," became an instant sensation.

People from all corners of the globe flocked to participate, immersing themselves in Amelia's world.

Tears streamed down faces as users interacted with virtual representations of Amelia and David, witnessing their love story unfold amidst the growing darkness.

The experience culminated with a performance of David's completed symphony, its powerful notes resonating within the virtual space, a call to action for a more just and equitable world.

The impact of "Echoes of Defiance" was profound.

It sparked a global conversation about the importance of preserving history, the dangers of censorship, and the role of art in fostering empathy and understanding.

Communities across the globe began hosting live performances of David's music, their renditions infused with the spirit of their respective cultures.

One evening, as Elise watched a group of young musicians from a war-torn region perform David's music, a tear rolled down her cheek.

The melody, born from oppression, had become a universal language of hope.

The once-silent violin case, now a symbol of unity, stood as a testament to the enduring power of art to transcend borders, languages, and even time.

As the last note faded, a young boy approached Elise, his eyes filled with a newfound determination.

"I want to learn the violin," he declared, his voice brimming with passion.

Elise smiled, a sense of deep satisfaction washing over her.

The legacy of Amelia, David, and the violin case wasn't just a story from the past; it was a living testament to the power of music to inspire future generations to raise their voices and create their own symphonies of change.

The melody, a whisper carried across time, would continue to echo through the ages, a reminder that even in the face of immense challenges, the human spirit's yearning for freedom and the transformative power of art would forever endure.

Chapter 19: A Whisper Across the Stars

The year is 2243.

Humanity has taken its first tentative steps beyond its cradle, establishing a small colony on a distant moon orbiting a gas giant.

Life on Kepler 186f-2b is harsh, a constant battle against the elements.

Yet, amongst the colonists, a spark of the past flickers – the melody from the violin case.

Dr. Evelyn Sharma, a descendant of Anya, the VR pioneer, leads the colony's cultural preservation efforts.

In her spare time, she tinkers with a battered old device – a relic unearthed from Earth's archives.

It's a phonograph player, a technology long obsolete but carefully preserved for its historical significance.

Evelyn cradles a worn record, its surface etched with grooves that hold a ghost of a song.

It's David Berger's symphony, painstakingly digitized from the original sheet music and Anya's VR experience.

With a tremor of anticipation, she places the record on the turntable, the needle hissing as it descends.

The room fills with the long-forgotten sounds of violins and cellos, a melody that carries the weight of history.

For the colonists, raised on synthesized music and the hum of machinery, it's a revelation.

A sense of wonder washes over them as they listen, transported to a world far away, a world once brimming with music and struggle.

The symphony becomes a regular part of colony life.

Evelyn shares stories of the violin case, of Amelia and David, their courage sparking a yearning for connection with their ancestral home.

The colonists begin composing their own music, inspired by David's defiance and the beauty they witness on their adopted moon.

Their compositions, a blend of the artificial and the natural, are infused with a melancholic longing for a planet they've never known.

One day, a routine communications check with Earth yields a startling discovery.

A faint signal, barely detectable, is picked up from a distant sector of the galaxy.

After weeks of analysis, the message is deciphered – a simple melody, a fragment of music with an uncanny familiarity.

Scientists recognize it – a portion of David Berger's symphony.

The realization stuns them.

Could there be another outpost of humanity out there, carrying the same melody across the vast expanse of space?

A wave of excitement surges through the Kepler 186f-2b colony.

They are not alone.

Evelyn, her heart pounding with anticipation, leads the effort to craft a response.

They record their own composition, a blend of David's symphony and their own music, a message of hope and resilience.

The signal, amplified by a powerful transmitter, is launched into the vast unknown, a whisper reaching out across the stars.

Days turn into weeks, then months.

Just as hope begins to dwindle, a faint signal flickers back.

It's a reply, a new melody woven from the familiar strains of David Berger's composition. Tears well up in Evelyn's eyes.

The violin case, a symbol of defiance and hope, had transcended planets and generations.

The melody, a whisper carried across time and space, had become a bridge connecting humanity across the vast gulf of the cosmos, a testament to the enduring power of music to unite us all, wherever we may be.

Chapter 20: Echoes in Eternity

Centuries had passed.

The Earth, ravaged by environmental changes, was a distant memory.

Humanity, scattered across a network of star systems, carried on their ancestral stories with reverence.

The legend of the violin case, a flicker of defiance from a bygone era, remained a cornerstone of their cultural heritage.

On a bustling space station named "Haven," nestled in the Orion Spur, a young musician named Kai strummed an ancient string instrument – a replica of the violin.

He had meticulously studied recordings and historical data, recreating the instrument's unique sound.

As his fingers danced across the strings, the familiar melody of David Berger's symphony filled the bustling marketplace.

The music, though foreign to most ears, held a captivating power.

Merchants paused their transactions, travelers stopped mid-stride, and children gathered around Kai, their eyes wide with wonder.

The melody transcended language barriers, its emotional depth resonating with the shared human experience.

Suddenly, a holographic figure materialized beside Kai.

It was Dr. Evelyn Sharma, her youthful face etched with the wisdom of centuries, beamed down from her research lab on a distant moon.

"Beautiful, Kai," her voice crackled through the comms, "The passion in your playing is truly remarkable."

A shy smile spread across Kai's face.

"Thank you, Dr. Sharma," he replied, bowing slightly. "The melody... it feels more than just music. It feels like a story."

Evelyn chuckled.

"It is, Kai. It's the story of Amelia and David, their love, their loss, and their fight for freedom. A story that reminds us of the fragility of our existence and the enduring power of art."

Over the next few days, news of Kai's performance spread rapidly.

People clamored to hear the music, their curiosity piqued by the story of a long-lost planet and the struggle for artistic expression.

Kai, overwhelmed by the response, decided to hold a concert in the Haven's grand central hall.

The day of the concert arrived, and the hall overflowed with people from across the station's diverse species.

Kai, illuminated by a spotlight, stood before the colossal audience, holding the replica violin.

As the first notes of David's symphony resonated through the hall, a hush fell over the crowd.

The music, though centuries old, spoke a universal language of love, defiance, and hope.

Tears streamed down faces, some in remembrance of a lost home, others moved by the sheer beauty of the melody.

In that moment, the hall transcended its physical space, becoming a shared space of human connection.

After the final note faded, a thunderous applause erupted, echoing through the vast station.

Kai, his heart brimming with emotion, took a bow.

He knew he wasn't just playing music; he was carrying a torch, a testament to the enduring human spirit.

Later, Dr. Sharma appeared backstage, her holographic form shimmering faintly.

"You see, Kai," she said, her voice filled with pride, "the melody from the violin case continues to inspire, even after all this time. It reminds us that music, like humanity itself, has the power to transcend time and space."

Kai smiled, gazing up at the vibrant ceiling of the hall.

He knew then that his responsibility extended far beyond mere performance.

He was a keeper of stories, a weaver of emotions, an echo of defiance that resonated across the cosmos.

The melody, whispered through generations and carried across galaxies, had become an eternal symphony, a testament to the enduring power of art to remind humanity of who they were, where they came from, and the unwavering spirit that would forever bind them together.

As long as the melody played, the legacy of the violin case, and the stories it held, would continue to echo through eternity...

Don't miss out!

Visit the website below and you can sign up to receive emails whenever Marquise The Coach publishes a new book. There's no charge and no obligation.

https://books2read.com/r/B-A-QBWDB-FFDBD

BOOKS 2 READ

Connecting independent readers to independent writers.

Did you love *The Forgotten Melody*? Then you should read *Mind Matters: Nurturing Mental Health and 20 Ways to Improve It*[1] by Marquise The Coach!

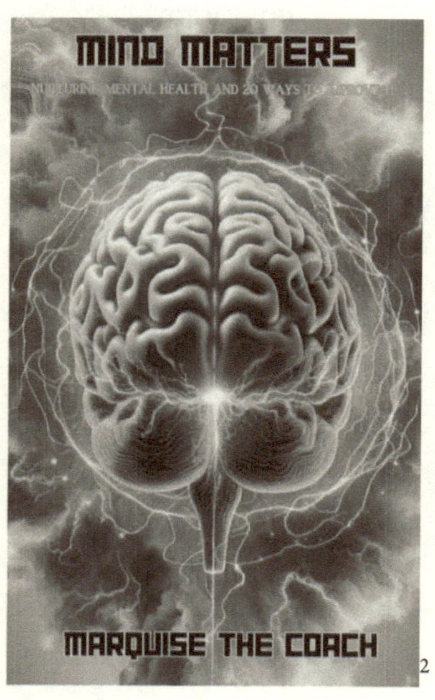

[2]

In today's busy world, it's more important than ever to focus on having good mental health. Many people feel stressed, worried, and overwhelmed, which makes them feel disconnected from themselves. In the middle of all the confusion, there's a chance for things to get better - a chance that you can find in the book "Mind Matters: Nurturing Mental Health and 20 Ways to Improve It" by Marquise The Coach.

Marquise is someone who has a lot of experience helping and supporting people with their mental health.

He knows it can be really hard for people to take care of their minds. Using what he knows from his own life and work, Marquise made a new

---

1. https://books2read.com/u/bQpDkP

2. https://books2read.com/u/bQpDkP

guide to help you take charge of your mental health and change your life for the better.

"Mind Matters" is like a light in the dark, reminding you that your mental health is important.

You have the ability to build strength, find balance, and do well. Marquise looks deeply into how our minds work and why we feel stressed or anxious.

"But "Mind Matters" is not just about knowing the problem - it's about finding answers. " In this book, you will find twenty helpful ways to make your mind and body feel better.

We've picked out a variety of techniques to help you feel better, from traditional practices like meditation and gratitude writing to newer methods like changing your thinking and setting boundaries. Each one is chosen to help you on your path to feeling good.

But what makes "Mind Matters" special isn't just how much it knows—it's the kindness behind it. Marquise cares a lot and always supports others. He helps people who want to start feeling better.

With Marquise by your side, you will go on a journey to learn more about yourself and become more strong and improve.

If you're tired of feeling stressed all the time and want to take control of your life, then "Mind Matters" is the perfect book for you. It will help you feel better and enjoy life more.

Let Marquise The Coach help you as you start a journey to heal, become stronger, and change. Take care of your mind and well-being. Let "Mind Matters" show you how to take care of it and grow.

Read more at https://marquisethecoach.com/.

T H E

MARQUISE

C O A C H

About the Author

As an author, coach, and advocate for holistic living, Marquise is on a mission to change lives—one mindset at a time. With a passion for inspiring mindfulness, awareness, and sustainable living, Marquise's journey is deeply rooted in a commitment to personal growth and societal well-being.

From a young age, Marquise felt called to make a positive impact on the world, driven by a profound sense of empathy and compassion for others. This innate desire led Marquise to pursue a path dedicated to understanding the complexities of the human mind and exploring innovative approaches to fostering well-being.

With years of experience as a coach and mentor, Marquise has witnessed firsthand the transformative power of mindfulness and awareness. By guiding individuals to cultivate a deeper connection with themselves and the world around them, Marquise empowers others to live authentically and consciously, making choices aligned with their values and aspirations.

In addition to promoting personal growth, Marquise is deeply passionate about sustainable living and environmental stewardship.

Recognizing the interconnectedness of all living beings and the planet we call home, Marquise advocates for mindful consumption, eco-friendly practices, and conscious living habits that honor the Earth and support future generations.

Through Marquise's writing, coaching, and advocacy efforts, countless individuals have found inspiration, guidance, and empowerment on their journey toward a more fulfilling and sustainable way of life. With unwavering dedication and a heart full of compassion, Marquise continues to make a difference in the world, one mindset at a time.

Read more at https://marquisethecoach.com/.

www.ingramcontent.com/pod-product-compliance
Lightning Source LLC
Chambersburg PA
CBHW060453160726
47992CB00003B/1204